The Squire's Little Girl

L. T. Meade

The Squire's Little Girl

Chapter One

The Squire's little daughter rode her pony down the avenue. She stopped for a moment at the gate, and the children at the other side could get a good view of her. There were four children, and they pressed together and nudged each other, and took in the small erect figure, and her sturdy pony, with open eyes and lips slightly apart. The Squire's daughter was a fresh arrival at Harringay. Her existence had always been known, the children of the village and the children of the Rectory had talked of her, but she had never come to live amongst them until now, for her mother had died at her birth, and her father had gone to live abroad, and Phyllis, the one child of his house, had been with him. Now he had returned; Phyllis was twelve years old; the Hall was open once more, full of servants and full of guests, and Phyllis Harringay rode her pony in full view of the Rectory children. Phyllis had a thick, rather short bush of tawny hair. Her eyes were of a grey blue, her little features were short and straight, and her small face had many freckles on it. She was by no means a pretty child, but there was something piquant and at the same time dignified about her. She stopped now to speak to Mrs Ashley, the woman at the Lodge; and the children pressed a little nearer, and Ralph touched Rose, and Rose nodded to Susie, and all three gazed at Edward with the same question on each pair of lips and in each pair of eyes.

"Shall we introduce ourselves," said Susie to her brother. "Do say yes, Ned; it is such an opportunity, and we are longing to know her. Do say that we may speak to her now."

But Ned shook his head. "It is not manners," he said; "we must not push ourselves on her. If, indeed, we could do anything for her it would be different."

And just then, as if to help the children in their darling wish, the white gates which led to the Hall refused to open at Phyllis's push, and Ned and Ralph both rushed to the rescue.

"Thank you," said Phyllis, with a toss of her head and a smile in her bright eyes. Then she paused and looked the boys all over. They were sturdy little chaps, and Ned in particular had the brightest brown eyes and the most honest face in the world.

"It is awfully dull, isn't it?" said the Squire's daughter. "I wonder how any one can live in a place like this. Are there more than two of you, and have you lived here always?"

"There are more than two of us," answered Ned, lifting his cap in the most polite manner, "and we don't find it dull. Here are my two sisters," he added; "may we introduce ourselves to you?"

"Oh, what a funny speech, and how nice it sounds!" cried Phyllis. "Four of you, and all children! I haven't spoken to anything approaching a child for a whole fortnight. If it wasn't for Bob here,"—she laid her hand on her pony's mane as she spoke—"I believe I should lose my senses."

"Well, you are all right now," said Ned, who certainly never lost his. "Here's Susie, and she's dying to know you; and here's Rosie, and I do believe she'd let her hair be cut short just for the pleasure of looking at you. And here am I, at your service; and I think I can promise that Ralph will do everything for you that boy could."

Phyllis's little face turned quite a bright pink. She glanced eagerly at both the girls, then she looked at Ralph, and finally she laughed.

"Let's be friends," she said. "I don't know who you are nor anything about you, but, oh, you are human beings, you are children! and I am so glad—I am so glad."

As she said the last words she held out her hand to Ned. He clasped it, and then let it drop, while the colour filled his own brown face.

"This makes all the difference in the world," said Phyllis. "What shall we do? How are we to spend the afternoon? You don't suppose, you four, that I'm going to lose sight of you, for if you do you are greatly mistaken."

"What shall we do? Where shall we go?" cried Susie.

She came close to Phyllis and looked earnestly into her face.

Susie was a very pretty little girl; she had bright black eyes and a quantity of curling black hair, and her cheeks were rosy like the soft bloom of a peach, and her lips when she opened them showed pearly-white teeth.

Phyllis looked right down into Susie's black eyes, and something in her heart stirred, so that the colour suffused her face, and she had difficulty in keeping back her tears.

"You are the Rectory children," she said; "please tell me what your surname is."

"Hilchester," said Ralph, without a moment's hesitation. "Oh! you will like father so much, Phyllis."

"And mother too," cried Rosie.

"Well, I tell you what it is," cried Phyllis. "I am going with you as far as ever you'll take me. Take me to the wildest and highest place in this neighbourhood, then I'll get off my pony and run; I want to run for bare life; I want to feel wild and free; I want to forget that I'm the Squire's little daughter, and that I've lots of money and grand dresses. I want to be, oh, *shabby*! oh, *wild*! dancing, joyful, just as if I hadn't a care in the world."

"Let's do it," cried Susie. "I know how; I know where. We'll take her to the Friar's Mount, won't we, Ralph? Oh, you may ride, pretty little Phyllis, but I don't think your pony can take you faster than we can run, and when we get to the Friar's Mount you'll know what freedom means."

"I should just think so," cried Phyllis. "I felt in prison until I saw you all, and now I'm so happy."

She touched Bob's neck with her whip, and soon she was cantering down the village street, the Rectory children following at her heels.

"Hullo!" cried a merry voice. "Where are you going, Phyl? Stop this instant, and tell me."

The words came from Squire Harringay. He was standing on the steps of the principal inn. He did not know his little daughter with her cheeks on fire, her eyes bright, her mane of hair standing out from her pretty neck, and four shabbily dressed but decidedly energetic children following her.

"Don't keep me now, Dad," was Phyllis's answer. "I've found playmates, and I am going to have a real good time. I'll tell you in the evening, but not now."

The gay little party turned a corner and were soon lost to view. The Squire turned to a neighbour—

"That's a pretty sight!" he exclaimed. "And who are those young termagants who, to all appearance, have made my little daughter lose her senses?"

"The Rectory children," was the response; "quite the wildest young imps in the countryside."

"Phyllis will be a match for them," said her father, and he rubbed his hands in a contented manner.

Chapter Two

Phyllis came home quite late. Her habit was torn; Bob, the pony, was covered with mud; mud had also been splashed all over the little girl's neat costume—even her face and hands were more or less disfigured by it. Her curly hair was disfigured too with the mud from the swamps and dirty roads over which she had passed, but there was a brilliant colour in her cheeks and a happy light in her eyes. She rode into the yard, and a groom came up to take her pony.

"Miss Phyllis," he exclaimed, "you have Bob in a lather!"

"Oh, never mind," said Phyllis; "I have had a jolly time. I have found playmates."

The groom touched his hat respectfully. It was the custom to be very respectful to the Squire's little daughter. She entered the house. Her governess, Miss Fleet, was waiting in the hall to receive her.

"Where have you been?" she said in a stern voice.

"Oh, Miss Fleet," cried Phyllis, "I have had such a time!—such fun, such delight! I met a lot of children, and I went up on to the hills with them. They are quite the most splendid children I ever came across in the whole course of my life. There are four of them—two boys and two girls."

"Don't you even know their names?" asked Miss Fleet.

"Yes, yes, of course. One is called Ned, and one Ralph; and there is a girl Susie, and another Rosie; and they adore me, and, oh, I am so happy!"

"You are very nearly late for dinner," said Miss Fleet, "and you are in a most disgraceful mess; it will take half-an-hour to clean you and make you respectable; and you missed your music-master. In short, you are a very naughty girl."

"I am a very happy girl," said Phyllis in the most contented voice in the world. "Please don't scold me, Miss Fleet; but I may as well say at once that I don't greatly care whether you are angry or not."

"Oh, don't you?" said Miss Fleet. "Do you suppose I am going to put up with such a very disobedient little girl?" Her voice was stern. She did not often scold Phyllis, for Phyllis, as a rule, was too good to be reprimanded. She followed her now to her pleasant bedroom. There Nurse was waiting to pet the little girl and make her presentable for dinner.

Miss Fleet looked into the room and said, "Here she is, Nurse, and I am extremely angry with her;" and then the governess closed the door and walked away.

Phyllis gazed at Nurse, her eyes brimful of laughter. Then she ran up to the old woman and said ecstatically—

"Oh! I am so happy, and I don't care a bit—not a bit—for what old cross-patch says."

"My dear Miss Phyllis," said Nurse, "you ought not to speak like that of your governess."

"Well," cried Phyllis, "she is cross-patch."

"I never heard you say that sort of thing before."

"I learnt it from the Rectory children. Oh, they are so nice—so very nice! I was with them all the afternoon. I am going again to-morrow, and the day after, and the day after that, and every day—every single day. Now, please, Nurse, help me to get tidy for dinner."

Nurse, who in her heart of hearts felt that Phyllis could do no wrong, assisted with right good-will to remove the mud-bespattered habit, and to get the little girl into her evening-frock. The Squire was immensely fond and proud of his little daughter, and she always dined in the evening with Miss Fleet and her father. Miss Fleet came downstairs first to the drawing-room.

"Where is Phyllis?" said the Squire.

"I am sorry to tell you, Mr Harringay, that Phyllis has been rather naughty. She has been out without leave, and came home just now in a disgraceful mess."

"The young monkey," said the Squire, laughing. "I saw her; she rode past the 'Blue Dragon,' a herd of children following her. I never was so amazed in my life; but she did look handsome and as if she were enjoying herself. I was told that the children belonged to the Rectory."

"I don't care whom they belong to," said Miss Fleet. "They are very naughty children, and badly behaved; and if Phyllis has much to do with them she will get just as rough and wild herself."

"Bless her! she is perfect whatever happens," said the Squire energetically.

"Mr Harringay," said the governess, "may I ask you a question?"

"My dear Miss Fleet, certainly. You know that I have the highest opinion of you."

"Have I the charge of Phyllis or have I not?"

"Bless me, bless me!" said the Squire, in some agitation, "of course you have the charge of her."

"Then that is all right; and she has got to obey me, has she not?"

"Of course, my good creature, of course." Just then Phyllis danced into the room. She looked very pretty in her evening-frock, and her happy afternoon had brought a red colour into her cheeks and a glow of happiness into her grey eyes.

The trio went into the dining-room, and Phyllis amused her father during dinner with accounts of Rosie and Susie and the two boys.

"I like the country," she said to her father; "I am glad we have come to live at the Hall; I am glad about everything. I am very, very happy to-night."

The Squire kissed her and petted her, and it was not until she was just going to bed that he broke a piece of news to her which she scarcely appreciated.

"My dear, it is good-bye as well as good-night."

"Good-bye, Father? Why?" asked Phyllis.

"Because I have to go to town to-morrow early, long before you are awake, my little daughter, and I shall probably not return to the Hall for quite a fortnight. But as you are so happy and have found friends, why, it does not matter so much, does it?"

"But I shall miss you," said Phyllis, little guessing how very, very much she was to regret the Squire's absence.

"I will write to you, pet, almost every day if I can; and if there is anything you fancy from town, you have but to say the word."

"I will write and tell you, Father. Are you prepared to give me quite big, big things if I want them?"

"I expect I am. You are my only child, and my pockets are pretty well lined."

"But big, big things for other people?" repeated Phyllis in an emphatic whisper.

"Come, Phyllis, it is time for bed," said Miss Fleet.

Phyllis gave her father another hug. Her eyes looked into his, and his eyes looked into hers, and there was no doubt that the Squire and his little daughter thoroughly understood each other. Then she danced away from him, and took her governess's hand and left the room.

"Miss Fleet manages her well," thought the Squire. "She is a very good woman, is very trustworthy and reliable, and the dear little thing wants a bit of discipline. Nothing will induce me to send Phyllis to school. I have the greatest confidence in Miss Fleet. I wish I hadn't to leave the child just now, but she is all right with the governess and Nurse—oh, and yes, there are the Rectory children; they see a lot of her, and she won't miss me, not a bit."

So the Squire went happily to bed and slept soundly, and went off at an early hour the following morning, kissing his hand as he did so in the direction of Phyllis's window.

Chapter Three

When Phyllis awoke the next morning she had the pleasureable sensation down deep in her heart that something very agreeable was about to happen. For a time she lay still, hugging the pleasant knowledge to herself. Then she sat up in bed with a laugh. Nurse had come into the room with Phyllis's bath, and was pouring the hot water out for her and preparing to help her to dress.

"Well, Miss," she said, "what is the matter?"

"Oh Nursey! those nice children from the Rectory are coming over to-day, and I mean to give them such a jolly time. The whole four are coming, and we mean to have hide-and-seek in the grounds and in the house. We'll be a bit wild and we'll be a bit noisy, but you don't mind, do you, Nursey?"

"No, darling," replied Nurse, "I don't mind; I am glad you have something to cheer you now that the Squire has gone."

"Oh, I forgot that!" said Phyllis. "I shall miss my darling father, but I am all the more glad that the Rectory children are coming."

Phyllis rose in high spirits, and presently she and Miss Fleet met in the schoolroom.

In the Squire's absence they were to have their meals in the schoolroom, and the table was laid now and placed in the cheerful bay-window, and the schoolroom maid was bringing in coffee, toast, and other good things for breakfast.

"I am hungry," said Phyllis.—"Good-morning, Miss Fleet."

"Good-morning, my dear," said Miss Fleet. "Take your seat quietly, please— not quite so noisily. Shall I give you a cup of coffee?"

"Yes, please," said Phyllis.

As a rule she rather resented Miss Fleet's remarks, but she was in such good spirits to-day that she determined, as she expressed it, to be extra well-behaved.

"I have been thinking, Phyllis," said the governess as she slowly ate her own breakfast, "that this is an excellent opportunity for us to begin a more exhaustive routine of work."

"Exhaustive routine? What is that?" asked Phyllis.

"I will explain to you. We have been going about for so many years that you have never settled properly to your studies. Your father has given me *carte blanche* to do exactly as I please with regard to your education. I mean to have the carriage this afternoon and to drive into Dartfield, the nearest large town, in order to see about new books for you, and also to get you music-masters, drawing-masters, and a dancing-master; you will probably have to join a dancing-class at Dartfield once or twice a week, and we may have to go there for your music. I, myself, will undertake your English education, and for the present will instruct you in French and German. We cannot quite arrange matters so as to fill up your time before Monday—this is Thursday—but on Monday I trust that we shall have a complete system so that every hour may be occupied."

"It sounds very dull," said Phyllis when her governess paused for want of breath. "Is there to be no time for play?"

"Play!" said Miss Fleet, with scorn. "You have played all your life. You want to work now."

"But 'all work and no play makes Jack a dull boy,'" said Phyllis in a flippant tone.

"Your uttering that remark, dear," said the governess, "shows how sadly you have been neglected. Of course you shall play after a fashion. You must take regular exercise, and have half-an-hour a day at gymnastics, and I may be able to arrange to take you to Dartfield for tennis and hockey according to the season."

"But why go to Dartfield for my games?" said Phyllis. "There are the Rectory children."

Miss Fleet opened her eyes. She did not speak at all for a moment; then she said gently—

"As we have finished breakfast, will you please say grace, Phyllis, and then meet me here in half-an-hour for lessons?" Phyllis muttered her grace in a decidedly cross voice. Miss Fleet immediately afterwards left the room. Phyllis went and stood by the fire. Suddenly she gave a little jump and her eyes danced.

"Why, of course I can't go with her—horrid old thing!—to Dartfield to-day," she exclaimed joyfully. "They are coming, the darlings, and I cannot be out of the way on any account whatsoever."

The remembrance that the Rectory children were coming cheered her immensely, and she danced gaily about the room putting things in order for Miss Fleet.

The moment the governess appeared Phyllis ran up to her.

Chapter Four

"Oh, you have brought all those horrid dingy books!" said Phyllis, seeing that Miss Fleet carried a huge pile of half-worn-out lesson-books in her arms.

"Keep away, Phyllis, a minute; I want to put them on the table," said the governess.

"What stupid things they are!" said Phyllis, forgetting for a minute the excitement which the thought of her little guests had given her, in her dismay at the appearance of the books.

She took up one volume after another, letting it fall on the table with an expression of great disdain.

"*Child's Guide to Knowledge,*" she said. "Horrid book. And oh! what is this? *Mrs Markham's History of England.* I hate *Mrs Markham.* Oh, and this—and this!—I say, Miss Fleet!"

"Phyllis, I wish to speak to you," said her governess.

"What is it now?" said Phyllis, but she was aroused by the tone.

She looked full up into Miss Fleet's small grey eyes, and her heart beat fast. For although Miss Fleet was really affectionate to the little girl, and was as a rule gentle, there were times when she could be quite the reverse. Phyllis saw that such a time had arrived.

"I wish to speak to you," said Miss Fleet. "During lessons you are to be industrious, careful, studious, and respectful. These books are not to be treated with levity; they are to be studied, and pondered over, and digested."

"Well, let's begin and get it over," said Phyllis.

She sat down by the table, drew a blotting-pad towards her and a bottle of ink, and looked up at her governess.

"And, oh, Miss Fleet! I want to say something. I can't go with you to Dartfield to-day."

"Why not, pray?"

"The four Hilchesters, the Rectory children, are coming here; I asked them yesterday. They are coming immediately after lunch, and they will stay to supper. I thought perhaps we might have supper in the evenings now that father is away. You don't mind, do you, Fleetie dear?"

"But I do mind very much indeed," said Miss Fleet. "What business had you to ask the Hilchesters without my permission?"

Phyllis bit her lips; her face grew scarlet.

"Well, I did, you know," she said.

"And extremely naughty you were. Did your father know that you had asked them?"

"I never told Dad; I—I forgot."

"Then you, a little girl of twelve years old, took it on you to ask a party of wild, disreputable, untrained children to this house without either his leave or mine!"

"Please, Miss Fleet," said Phyllis, who had a very quick temper when roused, "they are not disreputable and they are not wild."

"I repeat what I have said—disreputable, untrained children. I will have none of it."

"You cannot prevent it now—you daren't."

"Oh, we will see. Take this page of *Child's Guide* and learn it carefully. I will be back in a few minutes."

Miss Fleet went out of the room. Phyllis looked after her until the door was closed; then she gave a wild, sharp scream, and rushing to the window, looked out. From there she had a view of the stables, and presently she saw one of the grooms get on her own special pony, Bob, and gallop off. The groom carried a note in his hand.

"What are you doing, David?" shrieked Phyllis from the schoolroom window.

The man paused, turned round in amazement, and looked up at the excited child.

"I am going with a note to the Rectory, Miss; it is from Miss Fleet."

"Stop one minute."

Phyllis dashed to the table, seized a sheet of paper, scribbled on it, "Come and save me; I am in the claws of a dragon," folded the note, directed it to Ralph, and threw it out of the window.

"Take that note too to the Rectory," she said.

David picked it up, grinned from ear to ear, and galloped off.

When Miss Fleet returned she found Phyllis bending attentively over her *Child's Guide*.

"I hope you know it," said Miss Fleet.

"I have sent a line to Mrs Hilchester to say that it is not convenient for the children to come to-day. If you are very good I will ask the two girls to tea some afternoon when we have settled to our routine of work. Now don't say any more about them; attend like a good girl to your lessons."

"But I'm not going to Dartfield this afternoon," said Phyllis.

"You are if I desire it."

Phyllis shut up her lips. She could look very obstinate when she pleased. Her eyes now fixed themselves boldly on the governess's face, and her eyes seemed to say:

"I am hating you for being cruel; I am hating you right hard." But Miss Fleet was impervious to the flashing glances of her rebellious pupil.

Lessons went on after a fashion, and at last luncheon was announced. Miss Fleet and her pupil lunched in the library.

"Now go upstairs, Phyllis," said her governess, "put on your hat, and come down within a quarter of an hour. Tell Nurse to see that your gloves are in order; and you had better wear a jacket; it may rain."

Phyllis went out of the room without a word. Miss Fleet stood at the library door and watched the little figure as it mounted slowly—very slowly—the winding stairs.

There was something very naughty about that little figure just then, and yet at the same time something pathetic.

"Poor child! I am sorry I disappointed her," thought the governess; "but I have my duty to perform. I hear on all hands that the four young Hilchesters are the terror of the neighbourhood: so wild, so untrained, so disobedient. I should certainly be unworthy of the position I hold if I allowed Phyllis to have anything to do with them. Yes, I will keep my word, and the girls may have tea here in a week or so, but they shall not be alone with Phyllis; of that I am resolved."

Meanwhile the little girl, having turned a certain angle of the stairs, stood quite still, uttered a strange laugh, and then, turning quite aside from the nursery, ran down an unfrequented corridor and out into the back yard. She had already secured, in preparation for a certain adventure which she was fully resolved to have, a half-worn-out jacket and a torn and very dirty sailor-hat. She popped the hat on her head and fastened the jacket. Then she stood in the yard and looked around her. The only person within view was David the groom. Somehow, Phyllis expected to see David in the yard.

"Did you give the note?" asked the little girl, turning and speaking to him in an imperious way.

"Yes, Miss. I met the young gentleman all alone in the avenue, and I gave it him."

"And what did he say?"

"He only said, 'All right,' Miss."

"Thank you, David," said Phyllis; "I am very much obliged to you."

She ran across the yard and into a small fir plantation just beyond, and there she stood leaning over the railing. David could see her, and he smiled to himself.

"She is a spirited little miss," he thought. "Didn't Master Ralph show his white teeth just, when he read her note. His 'All right' meant all right, or I am much mistook. My word! the little miss will get into trouble if she ain't careful; but I ain't the one to split on her."

So when the pony-trap came round to take Miss Fleet and her small charge to Dartfield, nowhere could Phyllis be found. The whole house was searched, and the servants were questioned, but no one had seen the child.

Miss Fleet, in alarm, gave up her expedition and instituted a more vigorous search, but try as she would, nowhere could she or Nurse get a glimpse of the child. David, who alone knew the direction in which Phyllis had gone, had taken care to absent himself, and no one else had the slightest clue by which her whereabouts could be discovered. Presently Miss Fleet, in great anger, started off to drive to the Rectory.

"This really is intolerable," she thought. "I shall have to write to the Squire. Oh, of course, the naughty, naughty child has gone to those other wicked children. I shall have to give Mrs Hilchester a piece of my mind."

Chapter Five

Ralph Hilchester had never felt better pleased in the whole course of his life than when he got Phyllis's letter. That she should tell him that she was in trouble was more delightful to him than even a costly present would be— than even half-a-crown would be—and costly presents and half-crowns were rare treasures in the Rectory household.

His first determination was to tell his brother and sisters, but on second thoughts he resolved to keep to himself the delicious fact that Phyllis had written to him. He opened the blotted sheet of paper and looked at the words again:

"Come and save me; I am in the claws of a dragon."

"I should think I just will," thought Ralph; "it is exactly what I am made for. I always guessed there was something heroic about me. Fancy, in these prosaic days, having to deliver a princess from a dragon; I declare I feel exactly like Saint George of England."

So Ralph held his head very high, and, with the precious letter reposing against his heart, entered the Rectory. There dismay and indignation met him on every side.

"Oh Ralph," cried Rose, "what do you think? You know what a jolly afternoon we were all going to have!"

"Well?" said Ralph, his brown eyes dancing.

"Oh, you won't look quite so happy when you know! The Squire's little girl was nice enough yesterday, but she seems to have changed her mind. 'Other matters to attend to'—that is what that odious governess of hers said. Far too grand to notice us, of course."

"I wish you would speak plain," said Ralph. "I cannot get a scrap of sense out of that gabble of yours."

"How rude you are!" said Susie. "You will be as gloomy as us when you know. Well, it is this: we are not to go to the Hall this afternoon. We are not to play with Phyllis. It was the governess who wrote—that odious woman; she signed herself 'Josephine Fleet.' She says that Phyllis had no right to invite us, and we are not to come. Pretty cheek, I call it. Well, if Phyllis does not want us, I'm sure we don't want her."

"But that is all very fine," said Rosie; "I do want Phyllis. She promised me an old doll she had discarded, and she gave distinct hopes that we might have a baby-house of hers; and, anyhow, she is very jolly, and I did want to have a good time at the Hall. I call it horrid; I do indeed."

"And so do I," said Ned. "It is a precious big shame. But there, Ralph, we will go out rabbit-hunting this afternoon; I want to see if some of our snares have caught any."

"You are horridly cruel about rabbits; you know you are," said Rosie.

"Not at all; the sort of snare I have laid does not hurt any of them," said Ned. "Come along, Ralph, won't you?" But Ralph held back.

"Sorry I can't," he said; "other things to attend to."

He spoke in a lofty tone, and the feel of the precious letter in his pocket made his heart throb.

The Hilchesters were not a patient family, and they fell upon Ralph tooth and nail. He was mean; he was shabby; he was hard-hearted; he did not care a bit for their disappointment; but nothing, nothing they could say altered the lad's determination. They might amuse themselves: he had other fish to fry; he could not accompany any of them that afternoon. It was in vain to plead and catechise, and reproach and fight. Ralph stuck to his resolve. The early dinner at the Rectory was therefore a somewhat sorry affair, and Ralph was all too glad when it came to an end. He had now, if possible, to blind his very sharp sisters and brother. This was no easy matter. During dinner he made up his mind what he would do.

There were occasions when Ralph, all alone and unaccompanied, walked as far as Dartfield. Dartfield was five or six miles away. He announced gravely to the family that he was going on a long expedition, and then he went upstairs and brushed his hair, and washed his hands, and put on a clean collar.

"What can it mean?" said Rosie, who was watching him through the keyhole. "Ralph with clean hands! Something must be up!"

"Of course something is up," whispered Susie. "Oh Rose! he hears us. He will be down upon us with a vengeance. Let's fly!"

Just as Ralph opened the door they did fly, scrambling up to the attics, where they locked themselves in.

"They watched me, the monkeys. I must blind them," thought Ralph.

So he started off quite in the opposite direction from the Hall, and gained the high-road. Ned now shouted to his sisters to come and help to search for rabbits, and the girls, in high discontent, saw nothing for it but to obey. But Ralph was generally the ringleader of all forms of fun and mischief, and his absence made the rest of the party doubly depressed.

Ralph ran a whole mile in the direction of Dartfield; then looking cautiously about him, he doubled back, got into the wood, skirted it, and presently came within measurable distance of the Hall. To his disgust, he heard his sisters' and brother's voices as they rambled about the wood.

Suppose by any chance Phyllis met them first; she scarcely knew one from the other of the Rectory children so far. If she saw them she would think they had come to save her, and would rush to them and tell them all about her trouble. Ralph would indeed then be out of it. He quickened his steps therefore, boldly entered the wood, which was on Squire Harringay's property, and a moment later came face to face with the little girl.

She was leaning against the stile waiting for him. It had not occurred to her that he would come alone, but when she saw him, and noticed how tall and manly he looked, and how strong and well developed, her heart gave a bound of rapture. She ran to him, took both his hands, and laughed aloud in her glee.

"Here I am," said Ralph. "Of course I mean to save you; you were right to trust me."

"I thought I was," said Phyllis; "I felt that somehow yesterday. But where are the others?"

"Oh! the others," said Ralph. "I thought you wanted me alone."

"It is ever so good of you to come, but I should like you all best," answered the little girl. "But there, you have come, and I will tell you everything. Let us walk round by the back of the stables. If *she* sees us I am lost."

"She in other words is the dragon," said Ralph.

"Yes—Miss Fleet; and I quite, quite hate her now."

"Tell me all about it," said Ralph, and he tucked Phyllis's hand through his arm, and they sauntered slowly in the direction of the field which led to the back of the stables.

Meanwhile Miss Fleet, in dismay and indignation, drove straight to the Rectory. Mrs Hilchester happened to be at home. She was in a room which was very plainly furnished. At a large centre table the Rector's wife had spread bales of red flannel and coarse grey serge and unbleached calico, and was busy cutting out garments which were to be made up immediately for the poor of the parish. When she heard Miss Fleet's step, she did not trouble even to look round.

"Is that you, my dear?" she said.

"And have you come to help me? But you are very late."

"I don't know what you mean by 'my dear,'" answered the indignant governess, "but I have certainly never had the pleasure of speaking to you before, and I may as well emphatically say I have not come to help you."

Mrs Hilchester dropped her large cutting-out scissors, and turned and faced her visitor.

"I am sorry," she said abruptly; "I thought you were Mildred Jones; she promised to look in and do what she could. I have a heavy pile to get through before nightfall. As you are here, do you mind holding this unbleached calico while I divide it into yards?"

"Really,"—began Miss Fleet.

But indignant looks and even words were absolutely thrown away on the busy Rector's wife.

"Catch," she said, "and hold tight. If you have anything to say, you can say it while we are busy. No one who ever comes to the Rectory is allowed to waste time or to be idle. Thank you very much."

It was impossible for Miss Fleet not to hold the unbleached calico, and it was difficult for her to be quite as indignant and as dignified as she had intended to be in such a position.

"Why, really, this is most extraordinary," she said.

"Oh! pray, don't let go, or I shall have all my trouble over again."

Miss Fleet held tight to the calico, which got heavier and heavier as more and more yards were measured off.

"Now, for goodness' sake lay it gently on the table. Thanks; that is a help. Now, my good friend, what is your business? If I can help you I shall be pleased to do so; at present I don't even know your name."

"My name is Josephine Fleet."

"Ah, you are little Phyllis Harringay's governess. I received a somewhat extraordinary note from you before dinner."

"I am puzzled to know why you should think it extraordinary. Phyllis asked your children to spend the afternoon with her. I did not find it convenient to have them. I wrote to you plainly on the subject. You seem to be a frank sort of person yourself; you cannot, therefore, object to frankness in others."

"On the contrary, I admire it. Pray push that bale of red flannel across the table. Thank you."

"Oh! I cannot help to measure the flannel into yards," ejaculated the angry Miss Fleet.

"I don't require you to. Have you come here because you have changed your mind and wish the children to go to the Hall? But I am afraid I cannot find them now; they have dispersed. I always turn them out of doors, whatever the weather, in the afternoon. Pray, do tell me what you want, and—don't mind my being a little brusque—go—"

"You really are," began Miss Fleet, but she checked herself. "I have come here," she continued, "to ask you a question. Phyllis is not to be found anywhere. Is she—Mrs Hilchester—is she at the Rectory?"

"The Squire's little girl? Most certainly not. Do you suppose we would have her here against your will?"

"Well, I hope not. Where can she be?"

"My dear, good creature, how can I tell you? I have never set eyes on the child. Pass those scissors, please, and—yes, and that basket with the cottons. Thank you so much. Would you like to sew up a seam while we are discussing where the little girl can be? Ah, I see you are not willing to help. Well, well! good-afternoon."

Chapter Six

There never was a more angry woman than Miss Fleet as she left the Rectory that afternoon.

Certainly, Mrs Hilchester had not been sympathetic. It is true she had followed her visitor into the hall, and had said by way of reassuring her:

"You need not be at all alarmed about your little girl—my children are often out hours and hours at a time, and I assure you that I never dream of fidgeting; they eventually come home, grubby perhaps, and with their clothes in disorder, but otherwise safe and sound. Naturally, in the country your little girl will do as others do. Sorry you cannot stay to help me with my cutting-out, but as you cannot, good-afternoon."

Miss Fleet scarcely touched the hand which the Rector's good lady vouchsafed. She got into the pony-cart and drove rapidly away.

"What next, indeed!" she said to herself; "to compare Phyllis, who has been cossetted and petted all her life, to those wild, bearish children. I am certainly extremely sorry we have come to live at the Hall. If only the Squire were at home I should give him a piece of my mind; as it is it will be my duty to punish Phyllis most severely when she does return. Poor Phyllis! I don't wish to be hard on her, but still discipline at any cost must be sustained. Of course, she has returned long before now; but to have upset all my plans—a mere child like that!"

Miss Fleet had now returned to the Hall, and her first eager question was: "Is Miss Phyllis in? Has any one seen her, or does any one know anything about her?"

Alas! Miss Phyllis had not come back; no one had seen her—no one knew anything about her.

Miss Fleet now began to be really alarmed. She had not, as a rule, a vivid imagination, but certainly horrors now began to crowd before her mental vision. There was that deep pond just beyond the shrubbery. There were some late water-lilies still to be found on its surface. Suppose—oh! suppose Phyllis had gone to it and had tried to drag in the lilies, and had— Miss Fleet turned quite white.

Or suppose she had gone right outside the fir plantation, and had been seen and appropriated by the gipsies who were camping in the field just beyond. Altogether poor Miss Fleet had a sad afternoon, while Phyllis, the naughty and the reckless, enjoyed herself immensely. It sometimes does happen like that even in the lives of naughty children: they have their naughty time, and they thoroughly like it for the present.

Phyllis had been very angry, and had determined to take her own way; and now she was having it, and her laugh was loud and her merriment excessive. For she had not been long in the field at the back of the stables, and Ralph had not long been enjoying the sweet pleasure of her society all to himself, when three heads appeared above the hedge and three gay voices uttered a shout, and Susie, Rosie, and Ned dashed across the field.

"Oh! oh! oh!" said Susie, "now we know why he was smartening himself up."

"Didn't he scrub his hands just," cried Rosie, "and didn't we watch him through the keyhole!"

"Oh, shut up, shut up!" said Ralph. "Now that you have come I suppose you must stay; but it was to me Phyllis wrote.—Was it not to me you wrote, Phyllis?"

"Well, yes," said Phyllis. "Yours was the first name that I thought of, but I wanted you all. It is all of you I like best. Now you have come we will have a gay time."

"But where?" asked Rosie. "Are we to come to the house after all?"

"I wish we could," said Phyllis. "I do earnestly wish we could. Perhaps—perhaps it would be safe."

She stood for a minute holding her finger to her lips; then a bright light filled her grey eyes and smiles wreathed her lips.

"Could you go up one of the back ways, and take off your shoes, and slip upstairs and up and up?" she said in a tremulous whisper.

"Oh, couldn't we just!" said Rosie, her eyes nearly dancing out of her head.

"Then I think we can manage," said Phyllis. "All my toys are upstairs in the big, very big, big attic; and there is the baby-house that I said perhaps you could have; and there are the dolls' cups and saucers; and if only we could smuggle something to eat!"

"Something to eat!" cried Ned. "I can run back to the Rectory and bring a lot of things—a whole basketful. No one will know; Mother is at her cutting-out for the poor, and trumpets would not turn her attention. I can get the things—I can and I will."

"We must not let Miss Fleet know; she'll never, never think of looking for us in the attic," said Phyllis, "and it is so big and so very far away from all the other rooms that we won't be found; the only danger is your being seen when you bring the basket."

"I will go straight away this very minute," said Ned, "and you had better wait until I return."

"I know something still better than that," said Phyllis. "Why go to the Rectory? Why don't you go to the village and buy things there—nice unwholesome curranty and doughy things?"

"Oh, I say, scrumptious!" cried Rosie. "I'll go with him. No one will see us. But, oh, I say, Phyllis, we have not got a single brass farthing amongst us!"

Ralph's face turned very red; he felt awfully ashamed of Rosie.

"But I have," said Phyllis; "I always carry my purse about." She opened it. "There is a five-shilling piece," she said.

"And may we spend it all?" said Rosie, looking with almost reverence on the solid piece of money.

"Oh, rather! only do get very unwholesome things."

"I know the kind, trust me," said Rosie, and she and Ned set to running as fast as they could.

While they were away Susie and Ralph and Phyllis walked up and down, and talked in quite lady-like and gentlemanlike styles, and Phyllis described how Miss Fleet had brought in the dull lesson-books, and how she had tried to crush her bit of fun; and the other two laughed, and told stories on their own account, and said how cross they had been when that horrid letter had arrived.

"Only I knew your real mind," said Ralph, and he gave a protecting, admiring look at the little girl.

"I guessed you were very nice, Ralph," she replied, and she laid her pretty hand on his arm.

Thus the time while Rosie and Ned were away buying the unwholesome things went quite quickly; and when they returned bearing large paper parcels and mysterious-looking bottles, they all stole softly into the house.

Phyllis knew exactly how to get in by way of the old unused part. She took the others round to the door over which ivy hung, and instructed Ralph how he was to unfasten the tiny window, and then squeeze in and unbar the door.

This he did with the despatch of quite an accomplished burglar, and when the door was opened the other four figures came solemnly in. They were quite solemn and breathless now in their excitement. When they got inside, their boots were carefully removed, and Phyllis led the way. They went up some narrow stairs. These stairs led to the old tower, and by the tower was another rambling staircase, which conducted them to the attics. So at last there they were safe and sound, as Phyllis explained.

"We must be quiet, but not too quiet," she exclaimed, "for nobody ever comes to the tower, and nobody ever comes in by that entrance, and Miss Fleet may think for ever and ever before she can possibly imagine that I am having high tea with you four in the big back attic. Oh, perhaps we had better lock the door; but even that is scarcely necessary."

But the door was locked, and then began a time of wild mirth. The food from the village shop was as decidedly unwholesome as the most venturesome little girl could desire. The cakes were nearly leaden in weight, were richly stored with currants, and were underdone; there were awful-looking lollipops of queer shapes and quaint designs, and there was ginger-beer of the worst quality, and lemonade which had never made acquaintance with lemons. But what mattered that? The food thus acquired was all the sweeter because of that wicked little flavour of wrongdoing about it; and Susie and Ned had also supplied great bags of nuts and some very green apples, so that these young folks thought it really was a feast worth being dreadfully naughty to obtain.

They made a table out of some old boxes, and the cakes were cut, and the lemonade went pop, and the dolls' cups and saucers were brought into great requisition, and time went very merrily both for the naughty little girl and the Rectory children. After the meal came to an end Phyllis began to show the toys she no longer required—the rocking-horse, which her father had given her when she was four years old, and which she had ceased to ride, and the big, big, wonderful dolls' house which Susie, aged ten, still found one of the most fascinating things in the world.

"You can have them all over at the Rectory," said Phyllis, with the royal airs of a young queen. "You can send for them any day you like; and there is a box full of dolls over there, and a trunk of dolls' clothes. I don't want them—I don't care for those sort of things without playmates. I tired of them long, long ago, but you can have them."

"Oh, I say, Phyllis," cried Susie, and she put both her arms round Phyllis's neck, "can't you come and play with all the darling, lovely toys with playmates over at the Rectory?"

"Yes, I could do that," said Phyllis, looking wistful; "and I love you all," she cried. "I have been an awfully happy girl to-day if it were not for Miss Fleet."

Chapter Seven

When happy times are wrong and come to an end, one generally goes through some bad moments. This was the case on the special occasion which I am describing. Loud was the fun in the big attic, merry the laughter.

The rattling of dolls' cups and saucers, the popping of lemonade bottles, and the shrieks of mirth over each volley of wit had come to their height, when there came a loud knocking at the attic door. The knocking was immediately followed by the angry turning of the handle, and then by the excited voice of Miss Fleet.

"Open the door immediately, you bad, bad children!" she exclaimed.

"Oh Phyllis, can we hide anywhere?" said Susie.

"No, no, Susie," answered Phyllis; "we are found out, and we have got to pay for it. Well, I have enjoyed myself; haven't you?"

"If you don't open the door immediately," said Miss Fleet's voice again, "I shall have it burst open."

"Yes, children, open the door directly," said a sterner, older, graver tone; and then Ralph drew himself up, and Edward prepared for severe punishment, for it was the Rector's voice which now was heard.

"Give me the key, Phyl," said Ralph, turning to the little girl. "I will say it was almost altogether my fault."

"You will do nothing of the kind, for it is not true," said Phyllis.

She turned very white, and her lips trembled. She did not like the bad moment which lay before her, but on no account was she going to excuse herself. So she marched—"just as if she were a queen, the darling," said Susie, describing it afterwards—to the door and unlocked it, and flung it open, and stood with her hair hanging about her shoulders and her frock in disorder, facing the indignant but almost speechless Miss Fleet and the tall, burly figure of the Rector.

"Well?" said Miss Fleet. "Well, and what have you to say for yourself?"

"I know I have, been very naughty," said Phyllis; "I know it quite well, and,"—her eyes danced—"and I'm *not* sorry; no, I have had such a good time that I'm not sorry. As to the children of the Rectory, they are not a bit, not one scrap to blame. It was all my doing. I wrote a letter to Ralph when you forbade them all to come, for it was shabby of you; and, as you would not allow us to have tea properly downstairs, we had it here. That is all."

The Rector pushed past Phyllis and walked into the room.

"Come, children," he said. "Phyllis Harringay has made a very frank confession, and has tried to excuse you all; but I don't excuse you, for you must have known that you did wrong to come here."

"Of course we did, Father," said Ralph; "but at the same time," he added, "when a girl writes to you, you know, and asks you to help her out of a mess, what is a fellow to do?"

The Rector could not help smiling. "And oh, please, please, Mr Hilchester," said Phyllis, "do ask Miss Fleet to forgive me! Do, do ask her!"

"It will be quite useless," said Miss Fleet. "I am determined that you shall be well punished.—I am obliged to you, Mr Hilchester, for coming to help me. I was really in such despair that I had to get some assistance.—Come, my dear."

She took Phyllis's hand and dragged her from the room. Phyllis struggled; but Miss Fleet was a strong woman, and Phyllis had no chance. She left the four Rectory children behind her in the attic with all the delightful débris of the delightful feast, and went downstairs, down and down, into the proper part of the house, into the dull rooms and the dull routine of her life, knowing that she was naughty, and knowing that Miss Fleet had a perfect right to punish her.

Miss Fleet took her straight into the schoolroom.

"Here you stay," she said, "for the present. I will talk to you when you are calmer. You stay here until I let you out. I am too angry to speak to you at all just now."

Miss Fleet turned as she spoke, shut the door behind her, locked it, and went away with the key in her pocket.

"Well!" said Phyllis.

She said this word aloud. She had been angry; she had been excited; she had gone through what seemed to her every sort of emotion during the last few hours, and now things had come to this.

"If only Father were at home," thought the Squire's little girl, and then she sank down on an ottoman in the middle of the room and burst into tears.

Her heart was very sore. She had not been a good girl, but, oh! she had enjoyed herself.

"Why is it so nice to be naughty, and why is it that I can't feel sorry?" she said to herself.

She nursed with all her might and main hot anger against her governess, and for a long time succeeded. But the days were short, and by-and-by the light faded away at the windows, and there was only the firelight in the room. The fire was a good one; it had a guard in front of it. Phyllis went and poked it up; it blazed, and soon cheerful flashes of light fell all over the room. There was no lamp nor any other way of making a light. Phyllis crouched down near the fire and tried hard to think.

"I wonder when I'll *begin* to feel sorry," she said to herself. "In all the story-books when the children are naughty they are desperately, madly sorry afterwards, but I'm not one bit sorry—at least not yet."

She nestled down comfortably on the hearthrug. Presently she took a pillow from one of the sofas and put it under her head, and then blinking into the fire and shutting and opening her eyes, she dropped off to sleep. When she awoke she found that the fire was nearly out; she was stiff and cold, too, from lying on the rug. She started up, and could not make out where she was.

Presently, however, memory came back to her. How cruel of Miss Fleet to leave her like this! How wrong!—how more than wrong!

"If Father were at home I would tell him he was to send Miss Fleet away," said the little girl to herself. "She is a horrid, horrid woman; she makes me downright miserable. Oh, how dark it is! and there is no more coal in the coal-hod, and the fire will soon be out."

She stood up and shook herself, and then she took the poker and poked what fire was left into as good a blaze as she could manage; but it soon died away for want of new fuel, and the little girl, who was now very desolate and in very low spirits and very hungry, began thoroughly to feel her punishment.

"I won't stand it," she said to herself. "It is awfully unfair. She has no right to do it."

Phyllis ran to the door, shook it, and began to cry out:

"Open the door, please. Somebody come and open the door. I am here; Phyllis is here."

But nobody answered because nobody heard her. Suddenly she thought of the bell. She ran to it and rang it over and over again; but as Miss Fleet had given positive directions that no one was to approach poor Phyllis in her imprisonment, there was no reply. The fire was now very nearly out.

"Well," said Phyllis to herself, "at this rate she'll kill me. I'll be found frozen to death in the morning; and, oh, I am so hungry!"

But just then, before her physical sufferings could get any worse, there came a slow step on the carpet outside. The door was unlocked, and Miss Fleet, bearing a lamp in her hand, entered.

She laid the lamp on the centre table; she then went over and rang the bell. Phyllis stood facing her. Her face was tear-stained and very pale; her eyes flashed an angry light.

"I can run past you," she said, "and get out of this room."

"You can," said Miss Fleet, just glancing at her and then bending down to adjust the flame of the lamp, "but you won't."

A servant appeared at the door.

"Fill this coal-hod, Henry, and bring it up immediately; and tell Cook to send Miss Phyllis's dinner up. Be quick, please; the room is rather cold."

The man departed, having just dared to give a sympathetic glance at Phyllis before he left the room. He quickly returned with the coals. The fire was built up and blazed merrily. He then drew down the blinds and pulled the curtains across the windows, and a moment later reappeared again, bearing a little tray of delicious food.

"I declare," thought the child to herself, "I never knew before how nice a thing it is to eat. I *am* ready for my chop and fried potatoes. Oh! and I am glad I am having roast apples."

She sat down quite cheerfully to her meal; even Miss Fleet's presence scarcely annoyed her, so hungry was she and so glad to eat.

Chapter Eight

At last the meal came to an end. While Phyllis was eating it Miss Fleet sat near the fire.

She read, or pretended to read, the evening newspaper which had just been sent to the Hall.

Presently Phyllis got up, uttering a low sigh.

"Have you said your grace?" said Miss Fleet.

"Yes," replied Phyllis. "I said it in a whisper. What else do you want me to do?"

"*I* wish you to listen to me—to be attentive and no longer impertinent. I'm tired of punishing you. You have been a very naughty girl, but I am willing to forgive you and to restore you to my favour, provided you do what I wish."

"What is that?" asked Phyllis in a guarded voice.

"Come here, Phyllis."

Miss Fleet drew the little girl towards her. Her voice had softened; some of the severity had left it.

Phyllis was the kind of child to be easily touched by kindness—no one could drive her, but affection and love could always guide her. Miss Fleet almost caressed the small hand which Phyllis stole into hers.

"I hate not being friends with you," she said. "You have been my constant care and my constant pleasure for the last three years. Why do you suddenly turn against me?"

"I don't," said Phyllis. "I have always liked you—very well, that is; but you don't understand me."

"I'm not going to argue with you, Phyllis. You are only a little girl of twelve years old. I am three times your age."

"Three times twelve are thirty-six," said Phyllis under her breath. "She never let out her age to me before."

The fact that she knew Miss Fleet's enormously great age gave her a slight feeling of satisfaction.

"Yes," she said aloud.

"I must be kind to the poor thing; she is so very aged," was her inward thought.

"Yes, I quite like you when you talk softly," she said. "Go on, please."

"I cannot argue with you; I can but give you my opinion. You behaved badly to-day—so badly, so disgracefully that I cannot bring myself to speak of it. You did this in your father's absence—which made it, let me tell you, ten times worse; but I will forgive you and not tell your father if you make me a promise."

"What, Miss Fleet?"

"Wait one moment. You don't care to be always in this room, do you?"

"I hate being in this room. I hate being punished. I hate—I hate—I hate you to be cold to me. Do be nice to me again, Fleetie, for I'm quite too awfully miserable just now;" and the little girl flung her arms round Miss Fleet's neck and burst into bitter weeping.

After all, Josephine Fleet did love her wayward little charge. She kissed her once or twice and patted her on her arm, and then she said:

"Now for our conditions. I forgive and you promise."

"I promise!" said Phyllis.

"Yes."

"And if I promise, you'll never tell Father?"

"I will never tell your father."

"And you will let me go into all the rooms and play, and ride my pony, and do everything just as I did before—just as I did before?"

"Just as you did before."

"Then, of course, I'll promise, darling Fleetie. There is no doubt about it. If you'll let me do as I did before, I'll promise. Is it to learn a lot of history? It is to do my horrid— Is it? Is it?"

"It is none of these things, Phyllis. It is this. You must give me your solemn word, as a lady, that you will not speak or have any intercourse with the Rectory children until your father's return."

"What!" said Phyllis.

All the light went out of her small face and all the gladness from her eyes.

"I didn't think you'd be so mean, Fleetie," she said, and she went right away to the other end of the room and stood with her back to her governess.

Miss Fleet glanced with a queer sort of longing towards the little figure.

The little figure at the other end of the room looked pathetic; it looked lonely. Miss Fleet remembered certain words of the Rector's:

"I cannot see why you should object to the children playing with each other. Squire Harringay did not object; on the contrary, he was glad."

"Yes, yes," thought the governess; "and I would have allowed it in moderation, and doubtless it can be arranged in moderation when the Squire comes back. But Phyllis did wrong, and she must be punished in such a way as to make her feel it. I am forced to get this promise from her. I can take nothing else."

But all the time while Miss Fleet thought, she kept watching the little figure, and presently she saw the shoulders slightly heave, and she guessed that Phyllis was crying.

"It is very hard; I hate myself," thought the governess. "But I must, I must make her feel it."

It was just at that moment that Phyllis wheeled right round and came up to Miss Fleet and said quietly:

"If I cannot see them, may I write to them to say why?"

"I will write to them and give the reason," said Miss Fleet.

"May I not write my own self to Ralph, please, or to—to Susie?"

"I will write to them," said Miss Fleet gently.

Phyllis stood quite silent for a moment. Once again her shoulders worked suspiciously, and Miss Fleet noticed that her little chest heaved, but she kept back her tears.

"There's Susie," she said after a pause; "she would so like the baby-house, and the rocking-horse that I never ride on because I have no playmates, you know. May they be sent over to the Rectory? I promised that she should have them. Need I wait till Father comes back to keep my promise?"

"You had no right to make the promise."

"But mayn't they go? Please say yes."

"Not until your father returns."

Phyllis now stood, very calm and despairing, close to Miss Fleet.

"You want me to love you, but you make it very hard for me to do so," she said gently. "I'll tell you what I'll do. I'll promise for two whole days. If Father isn't back at the end of two whole days, my promise is at an end. I don't give you my word, as a lady, after two whole days. That is all. I will not make any promise after that, not for anybody."

Chapter Nine

Phyllis was so tired after her day of exciting adventure that she slept quite soundly. She had no bad dreams in her sleep, and when she awoke in the morning and looked round her pretty, cosy room—with Nurse standing not far off ready to wait on her, with a bright fire burning in the grate, and her bath and all her other comforts close at hand—she raised herself on her elbow and gave a sigh of content.

"How nice you look, Nursey!" she said.

"How that pretty dress becomes you! What a darling, dear sort of face you have, Nursey; and how much I love you!"

But as she said the last words her happiness was changed into a sigh, for memory had returned.

"Oh Nursey!" she said, with a sort of groan, "I had forgotten just for a minute. Oh! I was such a miserable little girl yesterday, and Fleetie was so angry; but I have promised her, and for two whole days I will keep my promise. Do you think by any chance Father will be back at the end of two days?"

Now, Nurse had no very keen love for Miss Fleet. To begin with, she was jealous of her. Before Miss Fleet came on the scene she had Phyllis all to herself. It was she who superintended the little girl's work and play; it was she who petted her and loved her and made her happy. With Miss Fleet's advent these things changed; and although the good woman was far too sensible not to know that it was right that her dear little lady should have the best instruction in the world, yet there were times when she did not think that Miss Fleet quite understood Phyllis; the present occasion was one of these. If Phyllis had slept soundly all night—had slept the sleep of absolute exhaustion—Nurse had often awoke, and once even, drawn by a low, deep sigh from the little sleeper, had got out of bed, lit a candle, and scanned the small white face with no little anxiety.

"If this sort of thing goes on she will do for her, sweet little darling," thought the nurse. "She wants to cram her dear little head with all sorts of useless knowledge, and never once, never for a minute to think that the lamb needs play and laughter and companions. Why, bless her! it did my heart good to hear her laughing yesterday, when she and those young romps found their way to the big attic. Well did I guess what they were after, the termagants, and small idea had I of telling madam where they were. I wonder now what I can do to cheer up my little pet!"

So when Phyllis the next morning had looked piteously at Nurse, and had asked if her father was at all likely to be back within two days, Nurse had put a large bath-towel over the can of hot water, had stirred up the fire, and then, going close to the little girl, had spoken.

"You tell me all about it, darling," she said—"all, every single thing about it. The Squire did not a bit want to go to London, but it was business took him there. Why do you want him to be back so mortal bad in two days' time?"

Phyllis's face turned first red and then pale.

"Because I made a promise," she said, then slowly, "and the promise hurts me awfully; but it was only for two days. If Father stays longer away I know I shall get very naughty again. Nursey, I mean to be naughty; I mean to be. I will have them back again, Nursey, and I will give them every sort of thing they want; and I will go and see them, and I will disobey her. Oh! it is horrid of me, but I have not kept back anything from her. She knows quite well what she has to expect; I have been fair to her, and she knows—it is for two days. It is what you call an—an amnesty—is not that a long word?—and it is just for two days."

"Oh, but, my pet, you ought not to be naughty, you know," said Nurse, who felt she must read a little moral lecture to her charge. "It is I, darling, who would like to give you companions and every other mortal thing you want; but there, my pet, the governess is set over you by the master, and I suppose you must obey her."

"For two days, yes," said Phyllis.

She did not say any more, but a very heavy sigh escaped her lips.

Nurse and she then plunged into the mysteries of her toilet, and at the usual breakfast-hour a very sprucely dressed, nice-looking little girl joined her governess in the schoolroom.

Meanwhile the children of the Rectory were having very varied opinions with regard to Phyllis. Rosie announced that she thought Phyllis quite the most captivating and beautiful little girl in the world; but Susie, who had been even more fascinated, announced gravely that she thought Phyllis, for all her fascinations, was in the wrong.

"It was delightful to steal up into the attic and have our stolen tea," she said, "and to be promised those lovely, most, most fascinating playthings; but all the same what a state she had that governess of hers in! And—well, anyhow, Rosie, I would not do that sort of thing to my own mother. I would not be deceitful to her, and have friends when she did not approve."

"As if that horrid Miss Fleet could be compared to our mother!" said Rosie somewhat hotly. "There, Sue, you are talking nonsense, and I am not inclined to listen."

As to the boys, they declined absolutely to discuss Phyllis; Ralph felt that he was in a sort of fashion Phyllis's chosen prince.

"We do not understand, and we cannot pretend to," he said. "She will see us again when the right time comes; there is nothing I would not do for her, of course, but I cannot talk of it."

Susie burst into a merry laugh, and Rose looked attentively at her brother. Ralph turned on his heel; he felt very like a knight of ancient romance, and Phyllis was the fair lady whom he was to rescue. He did not like to own it to himself, but he was very much hurt at the way things had gone, and very much puzzled with regard to Phyllis's extraordinary behaviour; and he wondered how things were going to end. At school that morning he was not quite so attentive as usual, and went down a place in his form, and altogether did his lessons in that unsatisfactory way which is the usual result of being absent-minded. Instead of joining his brother and Susie and Rosie for their usual walk, he slipped away by himself, and of course he went in the direction of the Hall. He often peered through the trees to catch a glimpse of the dear little figure of Phyllis dressed in its pretty brown, with her rosy cheeks and bright eyes. At last, to his great delight, he saw her walking by herself in the distance. She was walking slowly, and evidently was lost in thought. The sight of her was more than Ralph could withstand. He ran fast, and soon was standing breathless and excited by her side.

"Oh Phyllis!" he said. "Oh Phyllis!"

Phyllis turned at once when she saw him, and her rosy cheeks got white, and there came a very puzzled look into her eyes.

"Ralph," she said, "I cannot explain anything. You must go away. No, I cannot give you any message. I have promised, and I must—yes, I must keep my word. Perhaps some day you will know, and I can tell you. No, I won't say another word. Go away, please—please."

There was something not only entreating but also commanding in Phyllis's face, and Ralph knew at once that he must obey her. He turned, therefore, very disconsolately, walked about twenty yards, and then looked back.

"Have you anything to say?" he cried.

"No," she answered; "and I won't even speak if you ask me another question, for I have promised, and I must keep my word."

Chapter Ten

Nurse did not often take the bit between her teeth, as she expressed it, but the time had now come when, in her opinion, she ought to do so. Accordingly she made an excuse to go into the town soon after breakfast, and sent off a telegram on her own account to the Squire.

The little message was worded as follows:—

> "Dear Master,—If you cannot come back in two days, please send for Miss Phyllis to town. Urgent.—Nurse."

This rather startling telegram reached the Squire in London about the middle of the day. Now, it so happened that he had made arrangements not only not to return to the Hall in two days' time, but, further, to go with a friend on special and urgent business to Scotland. They would both be travelling about a good deal, and to have Phyllis with them would be absolutely impossible; so the Squire contented himself with writing a long letter to Nurse, and giving her an address which would find him in case of need, and enclosing a five-pound note, which was to be spent on any special thing which Phyllis liked best to have. He also wrote to Miss Fleet, not, of course, alluding to Nurse's telegram, but speaking with great affection about his child.

"You must be as good to her as ever you can," he said. "I need scarcely say that I know you will be. I am sorry to be so long away from the dear child, but she will have her little friends, and doubtless their company will do much to sweeten her life."

This letter Miss Fleet received the following morning. She read it deliberately. Phyllis watched her face all the while.

"Well," said Phyllis, who had been as good as gold on the previous day, "when is Father coming back?"

"He does not say a word about coming back, Phyllis. Oh yes, though; he says in his postscript that we must expect him when we see him."

"Then he will not be back to-morrow night?"

"Certainly not, dear. He is going to Scotland."

Phyllis's face turned very white. Miss Fleet looked full at her.

"My dear," she said, "you have pleased me much by your conduct yesterday, and I trust until your father's return you will be equally good; then I shall have a delightful report to render him."

Phyllis made no remark. She would keep her word, certainly, as far as it went, but to-morrow she fully meant to see the children of the Rectory. This night would end the second day of her promise; she would consider herself free the next morning. With all her faults she was a very honest child. She looked full at Miss Fleet now.

"I won't deceive you," she said. "I made you a promise, and I will keep it; but, please, you can understand that my promise ends to-night. I mean that when this time to-morrow arrives, I won't have made you any promise with regard to being good or bad."

As Phyllis uttered these words the governess's eyes rested on that portion of the Squire's letter which expressed satisfaction at his little girl's having companions to play with.

"If he knew," thought Miss Fleet, "what thoroughly naughty children they are, he would certainly approve of my determination not to allow Phyllis to have anything to do with them. Yes, I must be guided by my own common-sense in the matter."

Miss Fleet therefore now looked full up at the little girl, and said slowly and gently:

"All the same, I do not think you will make me unhappy while your father is away."

Some one called the governess hastily; she ran out of the room. Phyllis continued her breakfast, feeling extremely discontented.

"Oh, I do wish Dad would come back!" she said to herself. "It is more than horrid to have him away. What am I to do? I know he would not mind my playing with the children."

As these thoughts came to her, she saw her father's letter lying upon Miss Fleet's plate. Phyllis was a thoroughly honourable child, and she would not have read the letter for worlds, but just then, as if to tempt her to the uttermost, a puff of wind came in through the open window. The letter, written on thin paper, fluttered to the floor, and as Phyllis sprang to pick it up, her eyes fell on the very words she was not meant to see. She turned very white, and a look of resolution crossed her face.

"So Father approves. Then I am quite right, and I will disobey to-morrow," she thought.

She put the letter back on Miss Fleet's plate, and a moment later her governess came in.

"Fleetie," said the little girl, "do you know what has happened since you left the room? This letter was blown off your plate by a gust of wind. I jumped up to put it back again, and I saw the words in which Father said that he was glad that I had playmates, so after that of course you will not object to my playing with the Rectory children?"

Miss Fleet's face turned very red.

"Am I to believe this story or not, Phyllis?" she said. "Is it possible that you did not read the letter on purpose?"

"I have told you just the very exact truth," replied Phyllis. "You can believe it or not, as you please."

She then got up and marched out of the room.

"Dear, dear!" thought Miss Fleet, "how very difficult it is sometimes to know what is right!"

The rest of the day passed quietly, and Phyllis was still a model child. She did her different lessons to the absolute satisfaction of her governess, and the time slipped by quickly.

"We have had a happy day," said Miss Fleet as she kissed the little girl just before her bed-hour. "I hope it is a forerunner of many others just as happy." Phyllis looked full at her, but did not speak. Miss Fleet tried hard to read the thoughts which were behind those frank grey eyes. Presently the little girl left the room and went to bed.

The next morning she awoke very early. She had a curious sense of something delightful, and, at the same time, very disagreeable, which was happening. At first her memory would not serve her right, but then it rushed back, and she knew everything.

"I have been good for two days, and I have not promised to be good for another instant," she said to herself. "I can do what I like to-day, and Father wants me to play with the Rectory children."

She raised herself on her elbow and looked at a little clock on the mantelpiece. She wondered why Nurse had not come in to dress her as usual. The clock pointed to a quarter past seven. The first rays of the wintry light were streaming in at the window. Phyllis got softly up and washed herself after a fashion, got into her clothes, and before Nurse appeared on the scene was already out. She walked quickly in the direction of the Rectory; excitement filled her breast; she was intensely interested in what she was about to do. Should she by any chance meet Ralph! How glad she would be to spring to his side, and to say:

"It is all right now, Ralph. I have kept my promise, and we can play together quite happily this afternoon."

But there was no Ralph about; nor was there any Susie or Rosie. She presently reached the Rectory gates, and walked up the avenue. She had started out without her breakfast, and she was very hungry, and it occurred to her that she might ask Mrs Hilchester to give her something to eat.

"Of course, I cannot stay long," she thought. "I must be honourable whatever happens. I must be back with Miss Fleet in time for lessons. Then in the afternoon the children can come over to me, and we can have a real good time." But all Phyllis's gay resolves and all her plans for the afternoon were suddenly put a stop to by the appearance of a gentleman who was driving down the avenue. He stopped when he saw the little girl, and put his head out.

"Are you not Miss Harringay?" he said. "Yes; I thought so. Please, do not go up to the Rectory."

"Why not?" said Phyllis.

"I have just been there, and two of the children are not well. Pray, go home as quickly as possible. May I give you a seat in my carriage? It is rather early for a little girl like yourself to be out."

"No, thank you," answered Phyllis, with dignity.

She felt angry with the doctor, who had often seen her on her pony, and had recognised her at once.

What business had he to interfere? And if the children were ill, it was all the more reason why she should go and find out about them.

So she waited until his carriage had turned an angle of the avenue, and then, putting wings to her feet, ran up in the direction of the house. The hall door was wide open. She rang the bell. No one attended to her summons. She heard voices in the distance—the quick voice of Mrs Hilchester as she bustled about. Then a child came down the stairs—a child with a rosy face, and with marks of tears round her eyes. The moment she saw Phyllis she rushed to meet her.

"Oh, Phyl! Phyl!" she exclaimed. "It is Ralph, and he is very ill. We do not know what he has got, we don't; and the doctor does not know, but he thinks perhaps he has something bad; and Susie is ill too. Oh! her throat is so sore, and the doctor says—"

But what further Rosie would have uttered was fiercely interrupted. Mrs Hilchester came out and stood in the hall.

"Rosie," she said, "how dare you! Who is this little girl?"

"I am Phyllis Harringay," answered Phyllis stoutly. "And," she added, "I am very sorry to hear that Ralph is ill. Please, may I come and sit with him, and tell him funny stories, and amuse him; and may I see Susie? I am so fond of them both, and of Rosie too. Oh, please, please let me!"

Mrs Hilchester fairly gasped.

"Two days ago," she said, "you would not have come here. Two days ago you invited my children to go to you, and then sent a note telling them not to come. Two days ago your governess was here—a most offensive person— and now, now you come. Do you think we want you here? Go away at once—at once—and get your nurse to change your things, and— Here, I will write her a note. Go out, child, and stand in the open air. Oh, this is too distracting!" Mrs Hilchester disappeared into her little sitting-room. There she wrote a few lines, folded them up, sprayed them with a sanitas spray which stood near, and put them into an envelope. She gave the envelope to Phyllis.

"Take that back with you," she said, "and do not come near the place for the present."

"But I am so sorry," said poor little Phyllis, and her bright eyes filled with tears.

"There, dear, there; I know you mean all right. But go now, for Heaven's sake!—Rosie, my dear, come with me."

Phyllis and Rosie looked longingly one at the other for the world of things they could talk about, for the world of sympathy each could have shown to the other; but for a reason unknown to either little girl, it was dangerous for them to meet. Phyllis walked very sadly back to her own home; her mother took Rosie into the parlour.

"You and Ned are going to your uncle Joe's as soon as ever your father can take you," she said. "If you are at all ill, or you have the slightest headache, you are to be sent back here; but there is just a possibility that you may escape. And now, my dear little girl, don't go upstairs, and don't talk to any one as you have just spoken to poor little Miss Harringay. You were very imprudent. Did I not tell you that you were not to speak to any other child?"

"But, oh, Mother! she looked so sweet, and she did promise the rocking-horse, and the baby-house, and—and I could not help myself, Mother, I could not really."

"Well, don't cry, child. Sit down and eat your breakfast. God help us all, I only trust you have escaped infection, and that she, poor little girl! has not received it from you."

Mrs Hilchester left the room. Rosie sat down close to the fire; she did not like to own it to herself, but her head did ache just a tiny bit, and her throat felt dry, and it hurt her to swallow, and as to eating her breakfast, she could not even think of such a thing. Oh! it would be very dreary at Uncle Joe's, even though Ned would be with her. She would think all the time of Susie's burning eyes as she looked at her out of her little bed, and hear her cry for "water, water," as she, Rosie, had administered it to her at intervals all night; and however hard she tried to shut her ears, she would hear Ralph's groans in his sickroom close by. Oh, what was the use of going away? Of course, she was not ill, and it would be horrid at Uncle Joe's; and suppose—suppose Phyllis got ill! But of course she would not. Why should she? If only she might go and stay with Phyllis at the Hall? If only she could find her way to the attic where the rocking-horse and the baby-house were! But, of course, Mother would not agree to that.

"Rosie, wake up," said her mother; "you are half asleep, dear. Why do you not take your breakfast?"

"I am not hungry, Mother."

"Does your head ache?"

"Yes, Mother, a little."

"How is your throat?"

"It only hurts a very little. I am all right, Mother. Is that the cab at the door? Are we to go?"

"Wait a moment, my dear."

Mrs Hilchester went into the hall. Her husband was waiting to take Ned and Rosie away with him.

"Well," he said, "are the children ready? I really must be off; there is a wedding at twelve o'clock to-day, and it is some distance to my brother's."

"Rosie cannot go," said poor Mrs Hilchester.

"What! is she bad too?"

"I fear it; I greatly fear it. We cannot send her away until we are sure."

"Well, anyhow, Ned is all right. Jump into the cab, Ned, and let us be off."

Chapter Eleven

A very malignant form of scarlet-fever had showed itself already in the village, and the Rector's children were some of the first victims. To say that Miss Fleet was shocked when she received Mrs Hilchester's note would but lightly explain the state of that good woman's feelings. She was so horrified that she forgot to scold Phyllis for her act, as she termed it, of disobedience; on the contrary, she flew to the little girl and clasped her in her arms, and said in a broken whisper:

"We must pray for your little sick friends. Let us kneel down here at once and pray."

"Yes," answered Phyllis in some surprise.

Miss Fleet fell on her knees, and Phyllis clasped her governess's hand and looked up into her face.

What Miss Fleet said aloud was quite comprehensible to Phyllis and soothed her very much. She asked God that the sick children might recover, and she spoke of them with affection and again called them Phyllis's friends. But what she did not say aloud was perhaps the most earnest part of her prayer, for in that she asked God to forgive her for not being as kind and sympathetic to Phyllis and to the Rectory children as she might have been, and she implored of God most earnestly the precious, most precious life of the only child.

That day a telegram reached Squire Harringay in Edinburgh. It was from the governess this time, and its purport was so grave that he decided to return home that day. He turned to the friend with whom he was transacting business and said:

"I have just had rather a nasty shock. You know, of course, that I have only one child, my little Phyllis, the apple of my eye, as you may well understand. Well, some children, friends of hers, have contracted a very bad sort of scarlet-fever, and she has been exposed this morning to direct infection. I hope that God will be merciful, and that the child may have escaped. But I am best at home, Lawson, and will leave here by the next train."

Early the next morning Phyllis was made happy by the arrival of her father. He could not pet her too much, nor look at her too often, nor make enough fuss about her. Phyllis wondered why every one was now so kind, and why the children of the Rectory were spoken of as her dear little friends, not only by Nurse and Miss Fleet, but by every one in the house.

"But they were scarcely my friends. I mean—I mean," said Phyllis as she sat on her father's knee that evening—"I mean that I love them most awfully, but Fleetie did not wish me to love them. She would not have called them my friends; she did not until they got ill."

"When they recover you shall see plenty of them," said Mr Harringay; "and now, my darling, let us talk of something else."

But Phyllis was not happy unless she was allowed to talk of the Rectory children. She told her father everything—all about that picnic tea in the attics, and poor Rosie's longing for the rocking-horse and the baby-house.

"Could not they be sent to her—couldn't they, Father? She would be so glad to have them; even if she was ill and her throat was sore, she could look at the rocking-horse and perhaps play with the baby-house."

"No, no," said the Squire. "No, no; we will keep them until she is well. But I will tell you what, Phyllis; we will have that baby-house down to-morrow, and you shall furnish it in the nicest and most fashionable style. You and Miss Fleet shall go out in the afternoon and buy new furniture for the entire house."

"Yes, what a lovely idea!" said Phyllis, and the thought cheered her up.

But nevertheless she was very sad during the next few days. Those who loved her watched her with anxiety.

The children at the Rectory were very ill, and little Rosie especially was the one nigh unto death. There came a day when the doctor feared that little Rosie might not recover. It was Rose who had kissed Phyllis so passionately; it was Rosie who, if any one, had given the little girl the dreaded infection. Mr Harringay had a curious feeling that Phyllis's life hung on the life of Rosie. He spent the entire day going between the Hall and the Rectory to make inquiries.

"Very ill. Very bad. Quite unconscious. Scarcely any hope. May last till the morning; not sure."

Such were the varied bulletins. Mr Harringay did not dare to tell Phyllis how bad her little friend was. Ralph and Susie were already out of danger; it was Rose whose life hung in the balance. Early the next morning the Squire got up and went across the fields to the Rectory. He could scarcely bring himself to raise his eyes to see if the blinds were all down or not. He walked straight up to the door. There the Rector himself greeted him.

"Well, well?" said the Squire. "Speak, my dear friend; I can scarcely explain what I feel for you."

The Rector grasped his hand.

"Better news," he said; "she has slept for the last three or four hours; indeed, she is sleeping still. Both the doctor and nurse think that she may awake out of danger."

"Thank God!" said the Squire.

He went back home. Although he had not entered the house, he would not meet Phyllis until he had completely changed his dress. He came down to breakfast. If Phyllis had taken the infection she ought to show some symptoms that morning. But Phyllis's little fresh face looked as bonny and bright as ever, and her eyes were as clear and her appetite as keen. In a remarkable way the Squire began to feel the load which had rested so heavily on his heart begin to lift.

"Phyllis," he said, "Rosie has been very ill, but I think she will get better."

"Will God make her quite well if we ask Him?" said Phyllis to her father.

"Do ask Him, my child; do," said the Squire.

Phyllis rushed out of the room. She came back presently and sat down in a contented way to her breakfast. She ate with appetite.

"Are you not anxious, Phyllis?" asked her father.

"Not now," she said in a cheerful tone.

"I spoke to God, you know, and it is all right."

"Bless the child," said the Squire.

Late that day the news came that Rosie was out of danger.

"Then Phyllis was right," said the Squire. He caught his little daughter to his heart, and kissed her many, many times.

After all Phyllis did escape, and the three children at the Rectory got well. Ned did not sicken at all with the dreaded fever. When they were well enough the Squire himself insisted on sending them to the seaside. There they got strong and brown and bonny, and came back with as gay spirits and as fond of Phyllis as ever. It was a very happy day when the Rectory children and Phyllis met once more in the old attic. The Squire was in their midst this time, and there was no naughtiness anywhere about, and Phyllis had found playmates at last.

The End